Plan
Your Destiny

Ever After High™

The future is
yours to write ~~write~~
rewrite.

your destiny

THIS BOOK
BELONGS TO

ISBN 978-0-545-72365-7
EVER AFTER HIGH and associated trademarks and
trade dress are owned by, and used under license
from, Mattel, Inc.
©2014 Mattel, Inc. All rights reserved.
Published by Scholastic Inc. SCHOLASTIC and
associated logos are trademarks and/or registered
trademarks of Scholastic Inc.
10 9 8 7 6 5 4 3 2 1   14 15 16 17 18 19/0
Printed in China   68
First printing, September 2014

BELIEVE

With this planner,
Ever After is | just the BEGINNING. |
Your future is more than fate. You are
not cursed or charmed or required to
follow in your parents' footsteps.

(DESTINY) isn't written in
permanent ink. It's dreamed. Your
legacy is a spell you cast. A legend
you decide to make true.

It's up to you to choose your own
storybook fate and plan your own
destiny. Your Happily Ever After
starts (NOW.)

Apple White

Royal or Rebel:
Royal

Motto:
The Most Fabulous
One of All!

Storybook Legend:
*Snow White and the
Seven Dwarves*

**Storybook
Romance Status:**
Everyone at school
thinks she and Prince
Daring Charming
are dating. But just
because her storybook
legend ends with
them getting married
doesn't mean they're
an item, okay?

All About Me

Name: Rebecka Vaughn

Age: 14

Motto: Never Give Up

With my freinds.

My Story Would Be: I grew up as a nobody that nobody knew existed, and then I went way, way, way up to the top.

I am a Royal or a Rebel?: Rebel

What's Your Story?

Secret Heart's Desire: _____ a little! _____

I mustn't write it down ar

that is 100 Sum $.

Special Talent: Art wing

_____

♥

Favorite School Subject: Science

Someday, I Want to Be: An Art tech

Ecologist. arch d

♥

Raven Queen

Royal or Rebel:
Rebel

Secret Heart's Desire:
To conjure her own destiny!

Special Talent:
Casting spells. It kind of runs in the family.

Favorite School Subject:
Muse-ic class. What, you thought only princesses could sing power ballads?

Briar Beauty

Royal or Rebel:
Royal

Best Friends Forever After:
Apple White and Blondie Lockes

Favorite Place:
Anywhere there's a party! If she's going to sleep for 100 years, she needs to make each moment count now!

Favorite Song:
"You Don't Know You're Charming" by One Reflection

My Favorite Things

My Best Friends Forever After:

Chloe Sandeen, natie Updegrave,
Elizabeth Steiner, Jaeleen Adams.

Favorite Food: Any kind of seafood

Favorite Place: Knobel's

Favorite Song: How do I choose
Just one

Favorite Memory: My first kiss
on my first rolocoster and
The other one is my
aunts and uncle

Mischief
and
Madness

Silliest Thing About Me: Silly?

~~I wouldn't describe anything~~

about me as silly ♥

The Worst Mischief I Ever Got Into:

I won't say. Over my soft

when I

in School yet

Something Only My Friends Know
About Me Is:

If I told, it wouldn't be

only my friends that knew.

My Storybook-Perfect Party Would Be:

A sleep over at my house

with all my friends

cookies that look

like me!

Madeline Hatter

Royal or Rebel:
Rebel

Silliest Thing About Her:
She can throw a tea party any time, anywhere.

The Worst Mischief She Ever Got Into:
The time she accidentally gave her pet mouse growing potion in a boat on Mirror Lake.

Something Only Her Friends Know About Her:
She can speak fluent Riddlish!*

Riddlish is a unique language consisting of rhymes and riddles. It's usually only spoken in Wonderland, unless you've been cursed with a babble spell, or are generally mad by nature.

The True You

Something Surprising About Me:

Sadly... Nothing 3rd grade and only being 80 and pounds.

If I Could Have Any Pet, It Would Be:

Honestly... Just a cat.

My Secret Weakness: Who would let anyone know that!!?!

How My Friends Would Describe Me:

Aloof for the most part, sometimes bossy and overbearing with new people

How I Would Describe Myself:

Secretly sad, boring, artistic and kind.

Ashlynn Ella

Royal or Rebel:
Royal

Something Surprising About Her:
Even though she's a Royal, Ashlynn works part-time at the Glass Slipper shoe boutique. Even Royals need to learn the value of a hard day's work!

Loyal Pet:
Sandella, a phoenix. Just like Ashlynn, this bird rises from the ashes more beautiful than ever.

Oh, Curses! Secret Weakness:
Uncontrollable obsession with shoes. Whenever she sees a pair she Must. Have. Them.

It's What I Do

Favorite Sport: Swiming

My Wicked-Coolest Outfit: IDK,
I'm not into clothes that my
aunt Tala gave me

Sneakiest Ability: I'm don't
have one...

If I Could Go One Place Without Anyone Knowing, It Would Be:

To my BF's house for some
"alone" time. *waggles eybrows*

Cerise Hood

Royal or Rebel:
Rebel

Favorite Sport:
Running. It's the one sport where the only person she has to count on is herself.

Cloaked in Mystery:
Using her magic red cloak, Cerise can travel unseen through the shadows.

Darkest Secret:
Cerise is actually half wolf. But she keeps her true nature hidden because she's afraid people won't accept her for it.

Write Rewrite Your Destiny

Use these weekly-planner pages to keep track of your class schedule, homework assignments, after school activities, or anything you like!

Don't forget to save the date for these hexcellent events!

- ♥ Book-to-School Party
- ♥ The Beauty Sleep Festival
- ♥ Legacy Day
- ♥ True Hearts Day
- ♥ Thronecoming

Monday

there
but isnot

today

Tuesday

asb

asb

Wednesday

today I have to be ready
to read my own Native story
to symo for another note
to plo sightbook

Thursday

Friday

Saturday

Sunday

Monday

Tuesday

Wednesday

Thursday

Friday

Saturday

Sunday

Monday

Tuesday

Wednesday

Thursday

Friday

Saturday

Sunday

Monday

Tuesday

Wednesday

Thursday

Friday

Saturday

Sunday

Monday

Tuesday

Wednesday

Thursday

Friday

Saturday

Sunday

Monday

Tuesday

Wednesday

Thursday

Friday

Saturday

Sunday

Monday
Briar's Book-to-School party is this week!

Tuesday

Wednesday

Thursday

Friday

Saturday

Sunday

Monday

Tuesday

Wednesday

Thursday

Friday

Saturday

Sunday

Monday

Tuesday

Wednesday

Thursday

Friday

Saturday

Sunday

Monday

Tuesday

Wednesday

Thursday

Friday

Saturday

Sunday

Monday

Tuesday

Wednesday

Thursday

Friday

Saturday

Sunday

WEEK OF _____

Monday

Tuesday

Wednesday

Thursday

Friday

Saturday

Sunday

Monday

Tuesday

Wednesday

Thursday

Friday

Saturday

Sunday

WEEK OF _____

Monday

Tuesday

Wednesday

Thursday

Friday

Saturday

Sunday

Monday

Tuesday

Wednesday

Thursday

Friday

Saturday

Sunday

Monday

Tuesday

Don't forget to do your Crownculus homework!

Wednesday

Thursday

Friday

Saturday

Sunday

Monday

Tuesday

Wednesday

Thursday

Friday

Saturday

Sunday

Monday

Tuesday

Wednesday

Thursday

Friday

Saturday

Sunday

Monday

Tuesday

Wednesday

Thursday

Friday

Saturday

Sunday

Monday

Tuesday

Wednesday

Thursday

Friday

Saturday

Sunday

Monday

Tuesday

Wednesday

Thursday

Friday

Saturday

Sunday

Monday

Tuesday

Wednesday

Thursday

Friday

Saturday

Sunday

Monday

Tuesday

Wednesday

Thursday

Friday

Saturday

Sunday

The Glass Slipper is having a shoe sale this week.
Buy one slipper, try the second one on free!

Monday

Tuesday

Wednesday

Thursday

Friday

Saturday

Sunday

Monday

Tuesday

Wednesday

Thursday

Friday

Saturday

Sunday

WEEK OF _____

Monday

Tuesday

Wednesday

Thursday

Friday

Saturday

Sunday

Monday

Tuesday

Wednesday

Thursday

Friday

Saturday

Sunday

Monday

Tuesday

Wednesday

Thursday

Friday

Saturday

Sunday

Monday

Tuesday

Wednesday

Thursday

Friday

Saturday

Sunday

WEEK OF _____

Monday

Tuesday

Wednesday

Thursday

Friday

Saturday

Sunday

Monday

Tuesday

Wednesday

Thursday

Friday

Saturday

Sunday

WEEK OF _____

Monday

Tuesday

Wednesday

Thursday

Friday

Have you practiced your solo for Muse-ic class yet?

Saturday

Sunday

Monday

Tuesday

Wednesday

Thursday

Friday

Saturday

Sunday

WEEK OF _____

Monday

Tuesday

Wednesday

Thursday

Friday

Saturday

Sunday

Monday

Tuesday

Wednesday

Thursday

Friday

Saturday

Sunday

Monday

Tuesday

Wednesday

Thursday

Friday

Saturday

Sunday

Monday

Tuesday

Wednesday

Thursday

Friday

Saturday

Sunday

Monday

Tuesday

Wednesday

Thursday

Friday

Saturday

Sunday

WEEK OF _____

Monday

Tuesday

Wednesday

Thursday

Friday

Saturday

Sunday

Monday

Tuesday

Wednesday

Thursday

Friday

Saturday

Sunday

Monday

Tuesday

Wednesday

Thursday

Friday

Saturday

Sunday

WEEK OF _____

Monday

Tuesday

Wednesday

Thursday

Friday

Saturday

Sunday

Monday

Tuesday

Wednesday

Thursday

Friday

Saturday

Sunday

WEEK OF _____

Monday

Tuesday

Wednesday

Thursday

Friday

Saturday

Sunday

Monday

Tuesday

Wednesday
Remember to meet the girls in the Castleteria for lunch.

Thursday

Friday

Saturday

Sunday

Monday

Tuesday

Wednesday

Thursday

Friday

Saturday

Sunday

Monday

Tuesday

Wednesday

Thursday

Friday

Saturday

Sunday

Monday

Tuesday

Wednesday

Thursday

Friday

Saturday

Sunday

Ashley, Fr, Royal

NAME/ROYAL OR REBEL?

March, 28

BIRTHDAY

MIRROR-PHONE NUMBER

color   food   Number

FAVORITE THINGS

FAVORITE CASTLETERIA FOOD

SILLY QUOTE

LEGACY DAY SIGNATURE

Anthony Jr, Rebel

NAME/ROYAL OR REBEL?

BIRTHDAY

color   food

MIRROR-PHONE NUMBER

color   food   Number

FAVORITE THINGS

FAVORITE CASTLETERIA FOOD

SILLY QUOTE

LEGACY DAY SIGNATURE

NAME/ROYAL OR REBEL?

BIRTHDAY

MIRROR-PHONE NUMBER

FAVORITE THINGS

FAVORITE CASTLETERIA FOOD

SILLY QUOTE

LEGACY DAY SIGNATURE

NAME/ROYAL OR REBEL?

BIRTHDAY

MIRROR-PHONE NUMBER

FAVORITE THINGS

FAVORITE CASTLETERIA FOOD

SILLY QUOTE

LEGACY DAY SIGNATURE

NAME/ROYAL OR REBEL?

BIRTHDAY

MIRROR-PHONE NUMBER

FAVORITE THINGS

FAVORITE CASTLETERIA FOOD

SILLY QUOTE

LEGACY DAY SIGNATURE

NAME/ROYAL OR REBEL?

BIRTHDAY

MIRROR-PHONE NUMBER

FAVORITE THINGS

FAVORITE CASTLETERIA FOOD

SILLY QUOTE

LEGACY DAY SIGNATURE

Daniel

NAME/ROYAL OR REBEL?

BIRTHDAY

MIRROR-PHONE NUMBER

calor , food , Number ,

FAVORITE THINGS

FAVORITE CASTLETERIA FOOD

SILLY QUOTE

LEGACY DAY SIGNATURE

NAME/ROYAL OR REBEL?

BIRTHDAY

MIRROR-PHONE NUMBER

FAVORITE THINGS

FAVORITE CASTLETERIA FOOD

SILLY QUOTE

LEGACY DAY SIGNATURE

NAME/ROYAL OR REBEL?

BIRTHDAY

MIRROR-PHONE NUMBER

FAVORITE THINGS

FAVORITE CASTLETERIA FOOD

SILLY QUOTE

LEGACY DAY SIGNATURE

NAME/ROYAL OR REBEL?

BIRTHDAY

MIRROR-PHONE NUMBER

FAVORITE THINGS

FAVORITE CASTLETERIA FOOD

SILLY QUOTE

LEGACY DAY SIGNATURE

NAME/ROYAL OR REBEL?

BIRTHDAY

MIRROR-PHONE NUMBER

FAVORITE THINGS

FAVORITE CASTLETERIA FOOD

SILLY QUOTE

LEGACY DAY SIGNATURE

NAME/ROYAL OR REBEL?

BIRTHDAY

MIRROR-PHONE NUMBER

FAVORITE THINGS

FAVORITE CASTLETERIA FOOD

SILLY QUOTE

LEGACY DAY SIGNATURE

NAME/ROYAL OR REBEL?

BIRTHDAY

MIRROR-PHONE NUMBER

FAVORITE THINGS

FAVORITE CASTLETERIA FOOD

SILLY QUOTE

LEGACY DAY SIGNATURE

NAME/ROYAL OR REBEL?

BIRTHDAY

MIRROR-PHONE NUMBER

FAVORITE THINGS

FAVORITE CASTLETERIA FOOD

SILLY QUOTE

LEGACY DAY SIGNATURE

NAME/ROYAL OR REBEL?

BIRTHDAY

MIRROR-PHONE NUMBER

FAVORITE THINGS

FAVORITE CASTLETERIA FOOD

SILLY QUOTE

LEGACY DAY SIGNATURE

NAME/ROYAL OR REBEL?

BIRTHDAY

MIRROR-PHONE NUMBER

FAVORITE THINGS

FAVORITE CASTLETERIA FOOD

SILLY QUOTE

LEGACY DAY SIGNATURE

NAME/ROYAL OR REBEL?

BIRTHDAY

MIRROR-PHONE NUMBER

FAVORITE THINGS

FAVORITE CASTLETERIA FOOD

SILLY QUOTE

LEGACY DAY SIGNATURE

NAME/ROYAL OR REBEL?

BIRTHDAY

MIRROR-PHONE NUMBER

FAVORITE THINGS

FAVORITE CASTLETERIA FOOD

SILLY QUOTE

LEGACY DAY SIGNATURE

NAME/ROYAL OR REBEL?

BIRTHDAY

MIRROR-PHONE NUMBER

FAVORITE THINGS

FAVORITE CASTLETERIA FOOD

SILLY QUOTE

LEGACY DAY SIGNATURE

NAME/ROYAL OR REBEL?

BIRTHDAY

MIRROR-PHONE NUMBER

FAVORITE THINGS

FAVORITE CASTLETERIA FOOD

SILLY QUOTE

LEGACY DAY SIGNATURE

NAME/ROYAL OR REBEL?

BIRTHDAY

MIRROR-PHONE NUMBER

FAVORITE THINGS

FAVORITE CASTLETERIA FOOD

SILLY QUOTE

LEGACY DAY SIGNATURE

NAME/ROYAL OR REBEL?

BIRTHDAY

MIRROR-PHONE NUMBER

FAVORITE THINGS

FAVORITE CASTLETERIA FOOD

SILLY QUOTE

LEGACY DAY SIGNATURE

NAME/ROYAL OR REBEL?

BIRTHDAY

MIRROR-PHONE NUMBER

FAVORITE THINGS

FAVORITE CASTLETERIA FOOD

SILLY QUOTE

LEGACY DAY SIGNATURE

NAME/ROYAL OR REBEL?

BIRTHDAY

MIRROR-PHONE NUMBER

FAVORITE THINGS

FAVORITE CASTLETERIA FOOD

SILLY QUOTE

LEGACY DAY SIGNATURE

NAME/ROYAL OR REBEL?

BIRTHDAY

MIRROR-PHONE NUMBER

FAVORITE THINGS

FAVORITE CASTLETERIA FOOD

SILLY QUOTE

LEGACY DAY SIGNATURE

NAME/ROYAL OR REBEL?

BIRTHDAY

MIRROR-PHONE NUMBER

FAVORITE THINGS

FAVORITE CASTLETERIA FOOD

SILLY QUOTE

LEGACY DAY SIGNATURE

Dream Your Legacy

(Gabrella)
Gabby, Breight

NAME/ROYAL OR REBEL?

BIRTHDAY

MIRROR-PHONE NUMBER

FAVORITE THINGS

FAVORITE CASTLETERIA FOOD

SILLY QUOTE

LEGACY DAY SIGNATURE

NAME/ROYAL OR REBEL?

BIRTHDAY

MIRROR-PHONE NUMBER

FAVORITE THINGS

FAVORITE CASTLETERIA FOOD

SILLY QUOTE

LEGACY DAY SIGNATURE

NAME/ROYAL OR REBEL?

BIRTHDAY

MIRROR-PHONE NUMBER

FAVORITE THINGS

FAVORITE CASTLETERIA FOOD

SILLY QUOTE

LEGACY DAY SIGNATURE

NAME/ROYAL OR REBEL?

BIRTHDAY

MIRROR-PHONE NUMBER

FAVORITE THINGS

FAVORITE CASTLETERIA FOOD

SILLY QUOTE

LEGACY DAY SIGNATURE

NAME/ROYAL OR REBEL?

BIRTHDAY

MIRROR-PHONE NUMBER

FAVORITE THINGS

FAVORITE CASTLETERIA FOOD

SILLY QUOTE

LEGACY DAY SIGNATURE

NAME/ROYAL OR REBEL?

BIRTHDAY

MIRROR-PHONE NUMBER

FAVORITE THINGS

FAVORITE CASTLETERIA FOOD

SILLY QUOTE

LEGACY DAY SIGNATURE

NAME/ROYAL OR REBEL?

BIRTHDAY

MIRROR-PHONE NUMBER

FAVORITE THINGS

FAVORITE CASTLETERIA FOOD

SILLY QUOTE

LEGACY DAY SIGNATURE

NAME/ROYAL OR REBEL?

BIRTHDAY

MIRROR-PHONE NUMBER

FAVORITE THINGS

FAVORITE CASTLETERIA FOOD

SILLY QUOTE

LEGACY DAY SIGNATURE

NAME/ROYAL OR REBEL?

BIRTHDAY

MIRROR-PHONE NUMBER

FAVORITE THINGS

FAVORITE CASTLETERIA FOOD

SILLY QUOTE

LEGACY DAY SIGNATURE

NAME/ROYAL OR REBEL?

BIRTHDAY

MIRROR-PHONE NUMBER

FAVORITE THINGS

FAVORITE CASTLETERIA FOOD

SILLY QUOTE

LEGACY DAY SIGNATURE

Royals

Trust Your Heart

Keanu, Ani4ai

NAME/ROYAL OR REBEL?

BIRTHDAY

MIRROR-PHONE NUMBER

calor   , foed   Number

FAVORITE THINGS

FAVORITE CASTLETERIA FOOD

SILLY QUOTE

LEGACY DAY SIGNATURE

Isaac, Greves

NAME/ROYAL OR REBEL?

BIRTHDAY

MIRROR-PHONE NUMBER

calor   , food   Number

FAVORITE THINGS

FAVORITE CASTLETERIA FOOD

SILLY QUOTE

LEGACY DAY SIGNATURE

Jenaswoxer

NAME/ROYAL OR REBEL?

July 28

BIRTHDAY

610-597-7265

MIRROR-PHONE NUMBER

Calor phi pp Food Tocoos, Mumbers,

FAVORITE THINGS

FAVORITE CASTLETERIA FOOD

SILLY QUOTE

LEGACY DAY SIGNATURE

Isaac, Padaq

NAME/ROYAL OR REBEL?

May 15

BIRTHDAY

colorplus Foolchiness Number bo

MIRROR-PHONE NUMBER

calor Blue, food Chinesfced, Number log

FAVORITE THINGS

FAVORITE CASTLETERIA FOOD

SILLY QUOTE

LEGACY DAY SIGNATURE

NAME/ROYAL OR REBEL?

BIRTHDAY

MIRROR-PHONE NUMBER

FAVORITE THINGS

FAVORITE CASTLETERIA FOOD

SILLY QUOTE

LEGACY DAY SIGNATURE

NAME/ROYAL OR REBEL?

BIRTHDAY

MIRROR-PHONE NUMBER

FAVORITE THINGS

FAVORITE CASTLETERIA FOOD

SILLY QUOTE

LEGACY DAY SIGNATURE

NAME/ROYAL OR REBEL?

BIRTHDAY

MIRROR-PHONE NUMBER

FAVORITE THINGS

FAVORITE CASTLETERIA FOOD

SILLY QUOTE

LEGACY DAY SIGNATURE

NAME/ROYAL OR REBEL?

BIRTHDAY

MIRROR-PHONE NUMBER

FAVORITE THINGS

FAVORITE CASTLETERIA FOOD

SILLY QUOTE

LEGACY DAY SIGNATURE

NAME/ROYAL OR REBEL?

BIRTHDAY

MIRROR-PHONE NUMBER

FAVORITE THINGS

FAVORITE CASTLETERIA FOOD

SILLY QUOTE

LEGACY DAY SIGNATURE

NAME/ROYAL OR REBEL?

BIRTHDAY

MIRROR-PHONE NUMBER

FAVORITE THINGS

FAVORITE CASTLETERIA FOOD

SILLY QUOTE

LEGACY DAY SIGNATURE

Madison, Beis / Royal

NAME/ROYAL OR REBEL?

BIRTHDAY

60 - 882 - 3821

MIRROR-PHONE NUMBER

Color green, Food Salsbury Steak, Number 10

FAVORITE THINGS

befy-cheasy Nachos

FAVORITE CASTLETERIA FOOD

O.M.G.

SILLY QUOTE

LEGACY DAY SIGNATURE

Luckas Frits / Rebel

NAME/ROYAL OR REBEL?

April 3rd

BIRTHDAY

246-247-4143

MIRROR-PHONE NUMBER

Color green black, Food Salad, Number 4

FAVORITE THINGS

bery-Cheesy Nachos

FAVORITE CASTLETERIA FOOD

SILLY QUOTE

LEGACY DAY SIGNATURE

NAME/ROYAL OR REBEL?

BIRTHDAY

MIRROR-PHONE NUMBER

FAVORITE THINGS

FAVORITE CASTLETERIA FOOD

SILLY QUOTE

LEGACY DAY SIGNATURE

NAME/ROYAL OR REBEL?

BIRTHDAY

MIRROR-PHONE NUMBER

FAVORITE THINGS

FAVORITE CASTLETERIA FOOD

SILLY QUOTE

LEGACY DAY SIGNATURE

NAME/ROYAL OR REBEL?

BIRTHDAY

MIRROR-PHONE NUMBER

FAVORITE THINGS

FAVORITE CASTLETERIA FOOD

SILLY QUOTE

LEGACY DAY SIGNATURE

NAME/ROYAL OR REBEL?

BIRTHDAY

MIRROR-PHONE NUMBER

FAVORITE THINGS

FAVORITE CASTLETERIA FOOD

SILLY QUOTE

LEGACY DAY SIGNATURE

NAME/ROYAL OR REBEL?

BIRTHDAY

MIRROR-PHONE NUMBER

FAVORITE THINGS

FAVORITE CASTLETERIA FOOD

SILLY QUOTE

LEGACY DAY SIGNATURE

NAME/ROYAL OR REBEL?

BIRTHDAY

MIRROR-PHONE NUMBER

FAVORITE THINGS

FAVORITE CASTLETERIA FOOD

SILLY QUOTE

LEGACY DAY SIGNATURE

NAME/ROYAL OR REBEL?

BIRTHDAY

MIRROR-PHONE NUMBER

FAVORITE THINGS

FAVORITE CASTLETERIA FOOD

SILLY QUOTE

LEGACY DAY SIGNATURE

NAME/ROYAL OR REBEL?

BIRTHDAY

MIRROR-PHONE NUMBER

FAVORITE THINGS

FAVORITE CASTLETERIA FOOD

SILLY QUOTE

LEGACY DAY SIGNATURE

NAME/ROYAL OR REBEL?

BIRTHDAY

MIRROR-PHONE NUMBER

FAVORITE THINGS

FAVORITE CASTLETERIA FOOD

SILLY QUOTE

LEGACY DAY SIGNATURE

NAME/ROYAL OR REBEL?

BIRTHDAY

MIRROR-PHONE NUMBER

FAVORITE THINGS

FAVORITE CASTLETERIA FOOD

SILLY QUOTE

LEGACY DAY SIGNATURE

NAME/ROYAL OR REBEL?

BIRTHDAY

MIRROR-PHONE NUMBER

FAVORITE THINGS

FAVORITE CASTLETERIA FOOD

SILLY QUOTE

LEGACY DAY SIGNATURE

NAME/ROYAL OR REBEL?

BIRTHDAY

MIRROR-PHONE NUMBER

FAVORITE THINGS

FAVORITE CASTLETERIA FOOD

SILLY QUOTE

LEGACY DAY SIGNATURE

NAME/ROYAL OR REBEL?

BIRTHDAY

MIRROR-PHONE NUMBER

FAVORITE THINGS

FAVORITE CASTLETERIA FOOD

SILLY QUOTE

LEGACY DAY SIGNATURE

NAME/ROYAL OR REBEL?

BIRTHDAY

MIRROR-PHONE NUMBER

FAVORITE THINGS

FAVORITE CASTLETERIA FOOD

SILLY QUOTE

LEGACY DAY SIGNATURE

NAME/ROYAL OR REBEL?

BIRTHDAY

MIRROR-PHONE NUMBER

FAVORITE THINGS

FAVORITE CASTLETERIA FOOD

SILLY QUOTE

LEGACY DAY SIGNATURE

NAME/ROYAL OR REBEL?

BIRTHDAY

MIRROR-PHONE NUMBER

FAVORITE THINGS

FAVORITE CASTLETERIA FOOD

SILLY QUOTE

LEGACY DAY SIGNATURE

NAME/ROYAL OR REBEL?

BIRTHDAY

MIRROR-PHONE NUMBER

FAVORITE THINGS

FAVORITE CASTLETERIA FOOD

SILLY QUOTE

LEGACY DAY SIGNATURE

NAME/ROYAL OR REBEL?

BIRTHDAY

MIRROR-PHONE NUMBER

FAVORITE THINGS

FAVORITE CASTLETERIA FOOD

SILLY QUOTE

LEGACY DAY SIGNATURE

Raegan, Treskd, Rcyal

NAME/ROYAL OR REBEL?

ApriL, 21

BIRTHDAY

MIRROR-PHONE NUMBER

FAVORITE THINGS

FAVORITE CASTLETERIA FOOD

SILLY QUOTE

LEGACY DAY SIGNATURE

Rebecka / reble

NAME/ROYAL OR REBEL?

October 9th

BIRTHDAY

MIRROR-PHONE NUMBER

color fecahia, Food rablegen Number

FAVORITE THINGS

Salsbury steak

FAVORITE CASTLETERIA FOOD

SILLY QUOTE

LEGACY DAY SIGNATURE

NAME/ROYAL OR REBEL?

BIRTHDAY

MIRROR-PHONE NUMBER

FAVORITE THINGS

FAVORITE CASTLETERIA FOOD

SILLY QUOTE

LEGACY DAY SIGNATURE

NAME/ROYAL OR REBEL?

BIRTHDAY

MIRROR-PHONE NUMBER

FAVORITE THINGS

FAVORITE CASTLETERIA FOOD

SILLY QUOTE

LEGACY DAY SIGNATURE

NAME/ROYAL OR REBEL?

BIRTHDAY

MIRROR-PHONE NUMBER

FAVORITE THINGS

FAVORITE CASTLETERIA FOOD

SILLY QUOTE

LEGACY DAY SIGNATURE

NAME/ROYAL OR REBEL?

BIRTHDAY

MIRROR-PHONE NUMBER

FAVORITE THINGS

FAVORITE CASTLETERIA FOOD

SILLY QUOTE

LEGACY DAY SIGNATURE

NAME/ROYAL OR REBEL?

BIRTHDAY

MIRROR-PHONE NUMBER

FAVORITE THINGS

FAVORITE CASTLETERIA FOOD

SILLY QUOTE

LEGACY DAY SIGNATURE

NAME/ROYAL OR REBEL?

BIRTHDAY

MIRROR-PHONE NUMBER

FAVORITE THINGS

FAVORITE CASTLETERIA FOOD

SILLY QUOTE

LEGACY DAY SIGNATURE

NAME/ROYAL OR REBEL?

BIRTHDAY

MIRROR-PHONE NUMBER

FAVORITE THINGS

FAVORITE CASTLETERIA FOOD

SILLY QUOTE

LEGACY DAY SIGNATURE

NAME/ROYAL OR REBEL?

BIRTHDAY

MIRROR-PHONE NUMBER

FAVORITE THINGS

FAVORITE CASTLETERIA FOOD

SILLY QUOTE

LEGACY DAY SIGNATURE

NAME/ROYAL OR REBEL?

BIRTHDAY

MIRROR-PHONE NUMBER

FAVORITE THINGS

FAVORITE CASTLETERIA FOOD

SILLY QUOTE

LEGACY DAY SIGNATURE

NAME/ROYAL OR REBEL?

BIRTHDAY

MIRROR-PHONE NUMBER

FAVORITE THINGS

FAVORITE CASTLETERIA FOOD

SILLY QUOTE

LEGACY DAY SIGNATURE

NAME/ROYAL OR REBEL?

BIRTHDAY

MIRROR-PHONE NUMBER

FAVORITE THINGS

FAVORITE CASTLETERIA FOOD

SILLY QUOTE

LEGACY DAY SIGNATURE

NAME/ROYAL OR REBEL?

BIRTHDAY

MIRROR-PHONE NUMBER

FAVORITE THINGS

FAVORITE CASTLETERIA FOOD

SILLY QUOTE

LEGACY DAY SIGNATURE

NAME/ROYAL OR REBEL?

BIRTHDAY

MIRROR-PHONE NUMBER

FAVORITE THINGS

FAVORITE CASTLETERIA FOOD

SILLY QUOTE

LEGACY DAY SIGNATURE

NAME/ROYAL OR REBEL?

BIRTHDAY

MIRROR-PHONE NUMBER

FAVORITE THINGS

FAVORITE CASTLETERIA FOOD

SILLY QUOTE

LEGACY DAY SIGNATURE

NAME/ROYAL OR REBEL?

BIRTHDAY

MIRROR-PHONE NUMBER

FAVORITE THINGS

FAVORITE CASTLETERIA FOOD

SILLY QUOTE

LEGACY DAY SIGNATURE

NAME/ROYAL OR REBEL?

BIRTHDAY

MIRROR-PHONE NUMBER

FAVORITE THINGS

FAVORITE CASTLETERIA FOOD

SILLY QUOTE

LEGACY DAY SIGNATURE

NAME/ROYAL OR REBEL?

BIRTHDAY

MIRROR-PHONE NUMBER

FAVORITE THINGS

FAVORITE CASTLETERIA FOOD

SILLY QUOTE

LEGACY DAY SIGNATURE

NAME/ROYAL OR REBEL?

BIRTHDAY

MIRROR-PHONE NUMBER

FAVORITE THINGS

FAVORITE CASTLETERIA FOOD

SILLY QUOTE

LEGACY DAY SIGNATURE

NAME/ROYAL OR REBEL?

BIRTHDAY

MIRROR-PHONE NUMBER

FAVORITE THINGS

FAVORITE CASTLETERIA FOOD

SILLY QUOTE

LEGACY DAY SIGNATURE

NAME/ROYAL OR REBEL?

BIRTHDAY

MIRROR-PHONE NUMBER

FAVORITE THINGS

FAVORITE CASTLETERIA FOOD

SILLY QUOTE

LEGACY DAY SIGNATURE

NAME/ROYAL OR REBEL?

BIRTHDAY

MIRROR-PHONE NUMBER

FAVORITE THINGS

FAVORITE CASTLETERIA FOOD

SILLY QUOTE

LEGACY DAY SIGNATURE

NAME/ROYAL OR REBEL?

BIRTHDAY

MIRROR-PHONE NUMBER

FAVORITE THINGS

FAVORITE CASTLETERIA FOOD

SILLY QUOTE

LEGACY DAY SIGNATURE

NAME/ROYAL OR REBEL?

BIRTHDAY

MIRROR-PHONE NUMBER

FAVORITE THINGS

FAVORITE CASTLETERIA FOOD

SILLY QUOTE

LEGACY DAY SIGNATURE

NAME/ROYAL OR REBEL?

BIRTHDAY

MIRROR-PHONE NUMBER

FAVORITE THINGS

FAVORITE CASTLETERIA FOOD

SILLY QUOTE

LEGACY DAY SIGNATURE

Mrs. Zellner, Royal

NAME/ROYAL OR REBEL?

April 17

BIRTHDAY

610-791-2800

MIRROR-PHONE NUMBER

color purple   Jlopiter/Neptune?

FAVORITE THINGS

Pisza

FAVORITE CASTLETERIA FOOD

you have brains in
your head. You have feet in your
shoes. You can steer yourself any
direction you choose.

SILLY QUOTE

Mrs. Zellner

LEGACY DAY SIGNATURE

Jaquely

NAME/ROYAL OR REBEL?

BIRTHDAY

MIRROR-PHONE NUMBER

Color   Food   Number

FAVORITE THINGS

FAVORITE CASTLETERIA FOOD

SILLY QUOTE

LEGACY DAY SIGNATURE

NAME/ROYAL OR REBEL?

BIRTHDAY

MIRROR-PHONE NUMBER

FAVORITE THINGS

FAVORITE CASTLETERIA FOOD

SILLY QUOTE

LEGACY DAY SIGNATURE

NAME/ROYAL OR REBEL?

BIRTHDAY

MIRROR-PHONE NUMBER

FAVORITE THINGS

FAVORITE CASTLETERIA FOOD

SILLY QUOTE

LEGACY DAY SIGNATURE

NAME/ROYAL OR REBEL?

BIRTHDAY

MIRROR-PHONE NUMBER

FAVORITE THINGS

FAVORITE CASTLETERIA FOOD

SILLY QUOTE

LEGACY DAY SIGNATURE

NAME/ROYAL OR REBEL?

BIRTHDAY

MIRROR-PHONE NUMBER

FAVORITE THINGS

FAVORITE CASTLETERIA FOOD

SILLY QUOTE

LEGACY DAY SIGNATURE